Alicia
the Snow Queen
Fairy

A gift from the fairies for Amelie Ferguson

Special thanks to Rachel Elliot

Copyright © 2017 by Rainbow Magic Limited.

All rights reserved. Published by Scholastic Inc., *Publishers since 1920*. SCHOLASTIC and associated logos are trademarks and/or registered trademarks of Scholastic Inc. RAINBOW MAGIC is a trademark of Rainbow Magic Limited. Reg. U.S. Patent & Trademark Office and other countries. HIT and the HIT logo are trademarks of HIT Entertainment Limited.

The publisher does not have any control over and does not assume any responsibility for author or third-party websites or their content.

First published in the United Kingdom in 2015 as *Alyssa the Snow Queen Fairy* by Orchard U.K., Carmelite House, 50 Victoria Embankment, EZ4Y 0DZ.

No part of this publication may be reproduced, stored in a retrieval system, or transmitted in any form or by any means, electronic, mechanical, photocopying, recording, or otherwise, without written permission of the publisher. For information regarding permission, write to Scholastic Inc., Attention: Permissions Department, 557 Broadway, New York, NY 10012.

This book is a work of fiction. Names, characters, places, and incidents are either the product of the author's imagination or are used fictitiously, and any resemblance to actual persons, living or dead, business establishments, events, or locales is entirely coincidental.

ISBN 978-0-545-85201-2

10 9 8 7 6 5 4 3 2 1   17 18 19 20 21

Printed in the U.S.A.   40
First edition, January 2017

Alicia
the Snow Queen
Fairy

by Daisy Meadows

SCHOLASTIC INC.

The Fairyland Palace

Alicia's Tower

Rachel's House

Tippington Town

Jack Frost's
Ice Castle

Blue Ice Mountains

Tippington Park

Wintry weather's my domain.
I love the hail and freezing rain.
Alicia's magic makes me sneer.
The winter gloom should last all year!

I want the winter winds to bite
And folks to shiver day and night.
I'll steal her icy spells and then
The spring will never come again!

Find the hidden letters in the stars throughout this book.
Unscramble all 6 letters to spell a special Snow Queen word!

The Magical Snowflake

Contents

Dull December

"What an icy, gray December this is,"
said Rachel Walker, blowing on her
fingers and shivering. "I'm starting to
wonder if it will ever be Christmas!"

It was Saturday morning, and Rachel
was in her backyard with her best friend,
Kirsty Tate. They had come out to play a

game of ball, but sleet was coming down. Kirsty shivered, too, and buried her hands deep into her pockets.

"I'm really glad I'm staying with you for the weekend, but I wish the weather wasn't so horrible," Kirsty said.

"We had such awesome plans," said Rachel. "But nature walks and boating on the lake won't be much fun when it's so miserable and freezing. It looks as if we'll be spending most of the weekend inside."

"Never mind," said Kirsty, smiling at her friend. "We always have fun when we're together, no matter what we're doing."

"You're right," said Rachel, trying to forget about the dark clouds above.

"Let's go inside," Kirsty said. "I think it's starting to snow."

"Oh, really?" said Rachel, feeling more cheerful. "Maybe we can go sledding."

"I don't think so," said Kirsty. "I only see one snowflake."

She pointed up to the single, perfect snowflake. It was spiraling down from the gray sky. The girls watched it land on the edge of a stone birdbath.

"That's funny," said Rachel after a moment. "It's not melting."

Kirsty took a step closer to the birdbath. "I think it's getting bigger," she said.

The snowflake began to grow bigger and bigger. Then it popped like a snowy balloon, and the girls saw a tiny fairy standing in its place. She was as exquisite as the snowflake had been. Her blond hair flowed around her shoulders, and she was wearing a long blue gown, decorated with sparkling silver sequins.

A furry cape
was wrapped
around her
shoulders, and
a snowflake
tiara twinkled
on her head.

"Hello, Rachel
and Kirsty," said
the fairy. "I'm
Alicia the Snow
Queen Fairy."

"Hello, Alicia!" said Rachel.
"It's great to meet you!"

"What are you doing here in
Tippington?" Kirsty asked.

"I've come to ask for your help," said
Alicia in a silvery voice. "It's my job to
make sure that everyone stays happy in

winter—in both the human and fairy worlds. I went to visit Queen Titania this morning, and when I came home I got a terrible shock. Jack Frost had gone into my home and taken my three magical objects. Without the magical snowflake, the enchanted mirror, and the everlasting rose, I can't look after human beings or fairies this winter."

"Oh no, that's awful!" Rachel

exclaimed. "Is there any way that we can help you?"

Alicia clasped her hands together. "Please, would you come to Fairyland with me?" she asked. "Queen Titania has told me so much about you. When I discovered that my objects were missing, I thought of you right away. Will you help me find out what Jack Frost has done with them?"

Kirsty and Rachel nodded at once.

"Of course we will," Kirsty replied.

"Then let's go!" exclaimed Alicia, holding up her wand.

The Magical Tower

Glittering snowflakes burst from Alicia's wand like a fountain and landed on the girls.

"They're as light as butterfly kisses," said Rachel, laughing.

She and Kirsty had already shrunk to fairy size, and their glittery wings were fluttering, eager to fly. They felt a cool wind whirl around them, lifting them into the air. They were carried up toward the dark clouds with Alicia at their side.

"I think the world's getting even more gloomy," said Kirsty, looking down.

Sleet was driving down all over Tippington, and the girls were glad to be leaving the bad weather behind. Better yet, they were going to Fairyland!

Rachel and Kirsty were secret friends with the fairies, and they always adored the magical adventures they shared.

Swirling snowflakes surrounded them now, until all they could see was glitter. When the snowflakes cleared, they were standing beside a tall white tower, and they were wrapped in warm fluffy capes, just like the one Alicia was wearing. All around, as far as they could see, were tall blue mountains, topped with snow.

"Welcome to my home," said Alicia, smiling at the girls.

The tower walls were not solid like the walls of the Fairyland Palace. Standing close to them, Rachel and Kirsty saw that they were made of swirling snow.

"That's amazing," said Rachel.

She reached out to touch the wall. It felt cold and coarse.

"But where's the door?" Kirsty asked.

"There is no door," said Alicia with a laugh. "You just need to trust me."

She took their hands and led them forward.

"We're going to walk into the wall!" Rachel exclaimed.

But she remembered what Alicia had said, and she kept walking. Instead of hitting the wall, they all walked straight through it and into Alicia's home!

It was warm and welcoming, with thick rugs, a roaring fire, and big sofas covered in cozy, colorful throw blankets. Hundreds of tiny golden lights hung around the room in graceful loops. When

the girls looked up, they saw that the
walls of the tower were covered with
twinkling lights all the way to the roof.

"Why doesn't the fire melt the tower?"
Kirsty asked.

"It's a magical fire," Alicia replied. "I

know spells to make it easy to live in cold weather. I have lived here for a long time, you see."

"Where are we?" asked Rachel.

"We are in the most remote part of Fairyland," said Alicia. "I live among the Blue Ice Mountains, far beyond Jack Frost's castle. He had no idea that I even lived here until this morning. His goblins drove his carriage the wrong way, and he arrived here while I was at the palace. I knew it was him because

I saw goblin footprints in the snow. So he has my magical objects, and now both Fairyland and the human world are in danger."

"What do your magical objects do?" Kirsty asked.

Alicia waved her wand, and three pictures appeared in the air in front of the girls—a snowflake, a mirror, and a rose.

"The magical snowflake makes winter weather just right," she said. " The enchanted mirror helps everyone to see

the difference between good and bad.
The everlasting rose ensures that new life
is still growing underground, and that
flowers will appear again each spring.
Without them, winter will be miserable
for everyone, and my home will start to
suffer, just like the rest of Fairyland."

With another wave of her wand, the
pictures broke into tiny pieces and melted
away to nothing.

"What do you
mean?" asked
Rachel.

"Come with me
and I will show
you," said Alicia.

She flew upward,
and they followed
her, higher and

higher, until they passed through the roof and fluttered up into the snow clouds above.

"It's like flying through fluffy balls of cotton," said Kirsty with a giggle.

Alicia led the way, and the girls sped after her. Suddenly, there was a break in the clouds, and they saw that Jack Frost's Ice Castle was directly below them. They were flying in the direction of the Fairyland Palace!

Winter in Fairyland

As they flew closer to the palace, the snow clouds separated a little. When Rachel and Kirsty gazed down, they gasped in surprise. They had been to Fairyland in winter before and knew how snowy and beautiful it usually looked. But today the snow was streaked with mud. It looked hard and icy instead of soft and powdery. There were no fairies playing outside at all, and spiky icicles hung from their toadstool houses.

"I don't understand," said Rachel. "Why is the snow so dirty?"

"And why is it so cold?" Kirsty asked. "There's hail in the wind."

"It feels like needles on my face," Rachel said with a frown.

Alicia stopped and fluttered above a frozen pond. She looked worried and upset.

"This is happening because my magical snowflake is missing," she said.

"You see, it makes wintry weather beautiful and calm, and never too harsh or too cold. I share that magic across the human and fairy worlds, but Jack Frost has taken it all for himself. Now everyone else will suffer. Jack Frost's home will have pleasant, snowy winter weather, but Fairyland and the human world will have nothing but gray skies, solid ice, and muddy snow."

"That's really strange," said Kirsty. "Jack Frost usually loves the harsh ice and bitter cold. Why would he want his home to be snowy and calm?"

"I think we should go to the Ice Castle and try to find out," said Rachel.

Alicia nodded. "I hope that he is keeping my magical objects there," she said. "Do you think we can find them?"

"Of course we can," said Rachel. "We just have to figure out what he's planning—and stop him!"

It was strange for the weather to get better when they reached the Ice Castle. Fat snowflakes were floating down over the castle. When the fairies flew over the battlements, they saw goblin guards building snowmen.

"Look down there," said Rachel, pointing to a lawn in the castle gardens. A large group of goblins was gathered, sitting on garden chairs and swinging

their legs. The chairs were facing a small bandstand, where Jack Frost was sitting on a throne of ice.

"You've found him!" Alicia said. "Good job!"

Rachel, Kirsty, and Alicia fluttered to the ground and crouched behind a bush. Peeking around it, they could see that Jack Frost had a book in his hands, and he seemed to be reading aloud. Beside him was a table, and on the table was a glass case covered with a dome.

"Look!" said Alicia in an excited whisper. "Look inside the glass case!"

Rachel and Kirsty saw a single snowflake that was floating magically in the middle of the dome. It was perfect in every detail.

"Is that your magical snowflake?" asked Kirsty. "It's beautiful!"

"We've found it!" said Rachel, giving a little hop of triumph.

"Yes," said Alicia, her face falling. "But how are we going to get it back when it is being guarded by Jack Frost and all those goblins?"

The Snow
Queen Appears

The three fairies thought for a moment, but they couldn't think of a single idea. They looked around at the goblins. Some of them were listening to their master, but most were fidgeting and whispering to one another.

"What is Jack Frost reading to those goblins?" Kirsty asked.

They strained to hear, and caught a few words drifting toward them. "Gerda and Kay heard the church bells ringing and knew that they were home."

"I know that story!" Rachel exclaimed. "It's *The Snow Queen*—my mom always reads it to me at Christmas. But why is he reading it to the goblins?"

Just then, the story ended, and Jack Frost turned to the front of the book again. The fairies saw two of the nearest goblins fidget and lean toward each other.

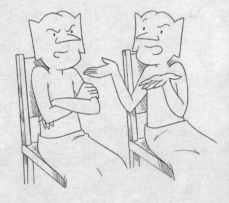

"He's going to read it again," said one with a groan.

"We've already had to listen to it

three times," grumbled the other. "I wish somebody would stop him!"

A goblin closer to Jack Frost stood up.

"Um, can we have a different story this time?" he asked. "I'm bored of that one."

"Boring! Boring!" chanted a few of the other goblins.

"Be quiet!" Jack Frost snarled at them. "I'm the boss, so you have to do what I say."

"What's the point of reading a book over and over again?" asked another goblin.

"And who cares about the Snow Queen, anyway?"

"You silly goblins!" Jack Frost yelled. "You wouldn't know a good story if it bit you on the nose!"

He almost threw the book at the goblin who was standing up, and then thought better of it.

"You need to learn about the Snow Queen," he said through gritted teeth, "because she'll be giving you orders very soon. She will rule everything with me, as soon as she sees that my powerful magic has turned everywhere else to treacherous ice. Together we will rule both Fairyland and the human world! She is the only one who can enjoy the cold as I can, so obviously she will want to find me. I am going to read about her until she arrives, and you will listen, like it or not."

"He doesn't know that *The Snow Queen* is a fairy tale," said Kirsty. "He thinks that there is a real Snow Queen—and he wants to rule the world with her!"

"*That's* why he's taken the snowflake," said Rachel. "He has used all its magic to make the Ice Castle snowy and beautiful, so that everywhere else is just ice."

As Jack Frost started reading the story again, Kirsty clasped her hands together and turned to Rachel and Alicia. "I've got it!" she whispered. "Alicia, could you make a snow queen out of ice? Something that could fool Jack Frost?"

"Certainly," said Alicia.

She flicked her wand, and a ribbon of ice shot from the tip. In a few seconds, it had formed an ice statue of a beautiful woman. She looked proud and haughty, and she wore a high crown and a set of flowing robes. She was very

beautiful, and she had one hand raised as
if she were waving.

The statue stood at the back of
the crowd of goblins, so it was a few
moments before Jack Frost spotted it.

He stopped reading at once and jumped to his feet, waving one hand and smoothing down his beard with the other.

"Welcome, Your Majesty!" he said, clearly groveling. "I am honored to see you in my frosty domain."

The goblins turned around and squealed with excitement.

"The Snow Queen is here!"

"I want her autograph!"

"What's she wearing?"

"I want to shake her hand!"

They leaped toward the frozen statue, and Jack Frost sprang after them.

"Don't crowd her!" he bellowed. "Show some respect!"

"Now's our chance!" said Kirsty.

While the goblins and Jack Frost had their backs turned, she and Rachel zoomed over to rescue the magical snowflake. But as they lifted the glass dome, an

unlucky gust of wind sent the snowflake
dancing through the air—straight toward
Jack Frost!

Rachel and Kirsty looked at each other
in alarm. They had to catch the snowflake
before Jack Frost noticed what was
happening!

Spinning Snowflake

"No!" cried Alicia.

She flew out from her hiding place, and the goblins and Jack Frost saw her.

For a brief moment, no one moved. Jack Frost stared first at Alicia, then at Rachel and Kirsty, and then at the Snow Queen ice statue.

"What?" he stammered. "Who…
how…?"

Another gust of wind made the
magical snowflake spin faster, and it
seemed to shake Jack Frost out of his
surprise.

"Get that snowflake NOW!" he roared.

The goblins flung themselves forward,
charging across the powdery snow,
their arms stretched out to catch the
snowflake. Several of them fell flat on
their faces and sank into the snow. Some
went in too deep and got stuck. Not
one of them could lay his hands on the
slippery snowflake.

Rachel and Kirsty darted toward the
snowflake, too, zigzagging around the
jumping goblins. The snowflake danced
above them, pushed this way and that
by all the hands flapping around it. Then

the girls heard an
outraged screech.
They turned to
see Jack Frost
holding the
hand of the
Snow Queen
statue. He
had tried
to shake her
hand and then
realized that she
was made of ice!

"I'll teach you to try to
trick me!" he shouted, glaring at Alicia.
"I'll make sure you've lost all your
magical objects forever!"

"I will not let you selfishly spoil winter
for everyone," Alicia declared.

"My goblins outnumber you three pests," Jack Frost cackled. "Any moment now they will catch your magical snowflake, and it will be mine!"

"That's never going to happen!" Rachel exclaimed.

Just then a goblin touched the snowflake. He batted it toward Jack Frost, who laughed and reached out to catch it. But one more gust of wind lifted it above his head, a little out of arm's reach. Still laughing, Jack Frost rose on his tiptoes, but this time the wind was lucky. The snowflake

was blown away from Jack Frost…and
straight into Alicia's arms!

"Hooray!" shouted
Rachel and Kirsty,
as Alicia twirled
upward, clutching
the snowflake
to her chest and
laughing happily.
Below, Jack
Frost shouted and
stamped in fury. He
kicked the statue and
then hopped around, holding
his toe and shouting.

Rachel and Kirsty flew up beside
Alicia as the snow in Jack Frost's garden
grew icy again, and new, crusty icicles
appeared on the castle.

"Look," said Alicia, pointing at the distant hills of Fairyland.

The muddy snow had turned to brilliant white, and they could see that some of the fairies had come outside to start a friendly snowball fight.

"It's a proper Fairyland winter again," said Kirsty with relief. "Thank goodness!"

"It's all thanks to you and Rachel," said Alicia. "I will return my magical snowflake to my tower and send you both home."

"But what about your other magical objects?" Rachel asked. "We want to help you get them back, too."

"Thank you, my dear friends," said Alicia, smiling at them. "That would be wonderful. I will come and find you again soon. But for now, good-bye!"

She waved her wand, and everything around the girls began to shimmer.

A few seconds later, they were standing once more in Rachel's backyard.

"What an exciting adventure!" said Kirsty, sounding a little breathless.

"The gray clouds are floating away," said Rachel, looking up. "The sun's coming out, too. We did it, Kirsty!"

The girls held hands and spun around in the winter sunshine.

"We just have to be ready to find the other magical objects," Kirsty said. "Jack Frost still has the enchanted mirror and the everlasting rose."

"We'll help Alicia get them back," said Rachel. "And I can't wait to see her again!"

The Enchanted Mirror

Contents

A Frosty Night

"It's another chilly evening," said Mr. Walker. "Let's light the fire."

Night had fallen, and a cold wind was rattling the windows of the Walkers' house. Rachel and Kirsty were curled up on the sofa with Buttons the dog between them. They watched Mr. Walker kneel down beside the fire, scrunch up some newspapers, make a pyramid of sticks, and add a match.

Soon, orange flames were leaping up from the grate, and the girls were feeling snug and sleepy. They sipped the hot chocolate that Mrs. Walker had made and smiled at each other. It had been a wonderful day. They had met Alicia the Snow Queen Fairy and helped her to rescue the magical snowflake from Jack Frost. Best of all, they felt sure that more adventures were on the way.

"This is what I love about winter," said Kirsty as the fire crackled. "Snuggling up beside a cozy fire makes up for all the cold weather."

Mrs. Walker glanced at the clock on the mantelpiece.

"Girls, don't go upstairs and get ready for bed," she said. "It's important that you get as little sleep as possible so that you will be too tired to play tomorrow."

Rachel and Kirsty looked up, feeling confused.

"Don't you mean that you *want* us to go to bed?" Rachel asked.

Mrs. Walker shook her head as if she had been daydreaming. "Of course you need to go to bed," she said with a puzzled expression. "I made a mistake."

Kirsty and Rachel made their way upstairs, feeling unsettled. As they were getting into their pajamas, Kirsty frowned.

"That was an odd mistake for your mom to make," she said. "Do you think it could have anything to do with the fact that Alicia's enchanted mirror is missing?"

"What makes you think that?" Rachel asked.

"Alicia said that the magic mirror helps

people think and see clearly," said Kirsty. "Maybe now that Jack Frost has it, everybody is getting confused."

Before Rachel could reply, the girls heard a tinkling noise. Then there was a faint tapping at the window, and they both jumped.

"Hurry, open the curtains!" said Rachel, feeling excited. "I think that might be magic!"

Together, the girls pulled open the curtains. The window was

covered in frost, in the most beautiful
patterns they had ever seen. There
were loops and swirls, delicate flowers,
and sparkling stars. Through a
snowflake shape, they saw a tiny,
beautiful face peering at them
and waving. It was
Alicia!

Rachel
opened the
window,
and Alicia
fluttered
inside. Her
long blue
gown was
sparkling with
frost as well as
sequins.

"It's nice to see you, Alicia!" said Kirsty. "But why are you out on such a bitterly cold night?"

"I'm here to ask for your help again," said Alicia. "Things are bad in the human world... and even worse in Fairyland."

"Is it because of your missing mirror?" Rachel asked.

Alicia nodded, tears glistening on her tiny eyelashes.

"People and fairies are getting confused between good and bad," she said.

"Rachel's mom got confused about bedtime earlier," said Kirsty.

"It will only get worse as long as Jack Frost has my enchanted mirror," said Alicia. "Some of the fairies are already in danger."

"What do you mean?" asked Rachel in alarm.

"Jack Frost is angry with me because I fooled him with the Snow Queen statue," Alicia explained. "He has used my enchanted mirror to trick some of the young fairies from the Fairyland School. He has made them go to work for him at his castle."

Rachel and Kirsty were horrified.

"Fairies working in the Ice Castle?" said Kirsty. "We have to do something to help them!"

Rachel nodded in agreement.

"Come to Fairyland with me now," Alicia said, stretching her arms wide. "Together we must stop Jack Frost and his mischievous plans!"

Fairies in Danger

Alicia raised her wand and smiled. Almost at once, Kirsty and Rachel felt warm all over, as if cloaks had been wrapped around them. They looked down and saw that they were shrinking to fairy size. Alicia had given each of them a long, fluffy coat with a snuggly hood, and their fairy wings were already fluttering on their backs.

Just then, they heard footsteps on the
stairs outside.

"It's my mom!" said Rachel. "She's
coming to say goodnight—we have to
go before she sees us."

"Don't worry,"
said Alicia, lifting
her wand again.
"Remember,
while you're in
Fairyland, time
stands still in the
human world. And
my magic will take you to
Fairyland in the blink of an eye!"

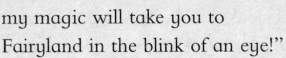

And as the girls blinked, they were
whooshed off their feet and twirled
around in the air. Their heads spinning,
they opened their eyes and found

themselves standing on the battlements
of the Ice Castle. Stars were glittering
above, lighting up two goblin guards
who were pacing toward them.

"Quick, hide!" Alicia whispered.

They darted behind a turret just in
time. The goblin guards walked right up
to it and paused.

"I don't like the night shift," said the tallest goblin. "It's too cold."

"You're just scared of the dark," said the second goblin with a snicker.

"Am not!" the tallest goblin shouted. "You're the one who ran away from your own shadow last week!"

Two more goblin guards appeared out of the gloom.

"Hey, you two lazybones," said one of them. "Why aren't you marching up and down?"

"It's too chilly for marching," said the tallest goblin.

"It's too chilly to be outside at all," said one of the others.

Behind the turret, Rachel had an idea. She whispered in Alicia's ear, and the Snow Queen Fairy nodded. She waved her wand and whispered,

"Winter treats for goblins four!
Snacks to eat and drinks to pour.
Let them guzzle, gulp, and gobble.
We'll sneak inside while they all
squabble!"

A single
sparkle of fairy
dust came
dancing out
of her wand
and made a

swirly loop toward the goblins. It hit the ground in front of them with a bang, and a camping stool instantly appeared with four sheepskin-lined chairs. On the table were four fuzzy scarves, four mugs of creamy, bubbling hot chocolate, and a tin of marshmallows. On the side of the box, in ice-blue writing, were the words, LOVE FROM JACK FROST.

"Hooray!" shouted the tallest goblin. "Jack Frost is the *best*!"

Rachel clapped her hands together in delight as the goblins hurried over to the table. Soon, all four of them were slurping the hot chocolate and cramming marshmallows into their mouths. They were so busy enjoying the treats that they didn't notice the fairies flutter past them. Rachel, Kirsty, and Alicia landed in front of the door that led from the battlements into the castle. It was locked and bolted.

"What should we do?" asked Kirsty with a groan.

"We won't let a little thing like a locked door stop us," said Alicia with a sudden grin.

She lightly touched the padlock on the door with her wand, and it sprang open. The chain dropped to the floor with a crash, and Rachel and Kirsty glanced around at the goblins, worried that they might have heard.

"Don't worry about them," said Alicia. "Those scarves are magical—they stop the wearer from hearing anything."

The door swung open and the three fairies flew in, listening for any signs of Jack Frost. Sure enough, they could hear a loud, angry voice from further in the castle.

"It's Jack Frost," said Rachel. "I'd know that voice anywhere."

"You fairies need to work harder!" they heard Jack Frost shout. "No stopping! No resting! Clean this castle from top to bottom!"

Rachel, Kirsty, and Alicia exchanged determined glances. They had to save the fairies!

Bewitched!

Rachel, Kirsty, and Alicia zoomed along
dirty hallways and down damp stairwells,
as Jack Frost's yells echoed around them.

"Which way is he?" asked Alicia,
covering her ears. "His voice seems to be
coming from all directions at once!"

"That way, I think!" said Kirsty,

pointing along a wide hallway. "It leads
to the Throne Room."

They flew a little farther, and stopped
when they came to a corner. The
shouting was very loud now. They peeked
around it and saw five young fairies on
their hands and knees in the hallway,
scrubbing the floor. Jack Frost was
watching them with his arms folded.

"Faster!" he shouted. "I want to be able

to see my face shining in this floor when I get back!"

He turned and strode away, his cloak billowing out behind him.

"Look at the pocket of his cloak!" said Rachel.

Five fairy wands were sticking out of his pocket.

"He's taken their wands!" Kirsty said in a horrified whisper.

Alicia darted around the corner and

flew over to the nearest fairy.

"We're here to rescue you," she said.
"Come with us!"

But the little fairy
shook her head.
"I'm happy
here," she said.
"This is really
fun."

Rachel
and Kirsty
fluttered over
to stand beside
another fairy.

"You're shivering," said Rachel. "You
must be freezing. Come with us, and
Alicia will use her special magic to
warm you up."

"Oh no, I love the cold," said the fairy,

her teeth chattering. "Please, leave us here. We want to stay with Jack Frost. He's so nice to us."

She tried to smile, but her eyes were full of tears. Despite her words, she seemed to be pleading with the girls. She looked very confused.

"It's as if they're saying the opposite of what they really feel," said Kirsty.

"They are," said Alicia in a serious voice, gazing into the fairy's eyes. "Try to remember," she said. "Did Jack Frost make you look into a mirror?"

The fairy nodded, then shook her head, then nodded again.

"Why would they agree to come here with him?" Kirsty wondered.

"They are very young fairies, and Jack Frost has used the enchanted mirror to confuse and bewitch them," said Alicia. "They won't see him clearly until the enchanted mirror is back where it belongs—with me!"

"We have to help them," said Rachel. "I can't bear to see them doing all this work for ungrateful Jack Frost."

"Until I have my mirror back, no one in the human or fairy worlds will be able to tell the difference between good and bad," said Alicia. "The fairies will not want to leave the Ice Castle. To help them, we have to find Jack Frost and take back my mirror!"

It felt awful leaving the five fairies scrubbing the floor, but they had to find Jack Frost. They flew as fast as they could, and caught a glimpse of him just outside the Throne Room. Kirsty looked at the wands in his pocket and frowned.

"There is something else in his pocket with the wands," she said.

"I can see a silver handle," Rachel added, as Jack Frost went through the door.

"My enchanted mirror has a silver handle," said Alicia.

"Maybe we've found it! Hurry, girls!"

They zoomed after him and darted through the door just before it closed. Jack Frost was sitting bolt upright on his throne, glaring at three young fairies who were hovering in front of him. Their hands were clasped behind them. There were no goblins to be seen. Rachel, Kirsty, and Alicia slipped out of sight behind a long curtain.

"I want your wands," Jack Frost was saying to the fairies, holding out his hand. "Give them to me now!"

The fairies did as they were told, and Jack Frost shoved the wands into his pocket. As he did so, Alicia saw the silver handle and nodded.

"That's my enchanted mirror!" she whispered.

Turning Up the Heat

"You are my new servants," Jack Frost
told the young fairies. "I'm fed up with
goblins. I want one of you to get a pen
and some paper—I'm going to write a
book about how I defeated you and took
over Fairyland. Write down everything I
say, and don't miss a single word or you'll
be in big trouble!"

The smallest fairy curtsied. She then rushed off to find a pen and a scroll. "I'm ready," she said.

"Once, a lot of pesky fairies ruled Fairyland," Jack Frost began. "But then something wonderful happened. Me! With my amazing magic, I controlled all the fairies and told them what to do. Here's how I did it…"

"He's so interested in the sound of his own voice, he might not notice if I take the mirror," Kirsty whispered.

"Be careful!" Alicia exclaimed.

Kirsty nodded, and fluttered over to stand behind the throne. Rachel and Alicia watched and held their breath as Kirsty reached toward Jack Frost's pocket. She was almost touching the handle of the enchanted mirror!

Jack Frost shivered and pulled his cloak tightly around him. Now the pocket was out of Kirsty's reach. She flew back behind the curtain, and Rachel squeezed her hand.

"Maybe if the room were warmer, he would take off his cloak," she said.

"Could you make it warmer in here, Alicia?" Kirsty asked.

As Alicia flourished her wand, shimmering hot air streamed out of it, coiling and swirling around the room. Jack Frost was so busy talking

about himself, he didn't notice that the
Throne Room was getting warmer …
and warmer … and warmer.

"I don't like to boast," Jack Frost was
saying, "but I have the biggest brain in
the whole universe, and it was only a
matter of time before I found a way to
take all the power
from Queen
Titania
and King
Oberon."
His
cloak
fell open
and then
slipped
to the floor
behind the throne.

"Now!" Alicia
whispered.

They
darted over
to the
cloak and
shook it,
searching
for the
pocket. But
the wands
fell out, clicking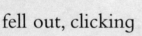
against one another. The girls heard
the sound of Jack Frost sucking air in
between his teeth. They looked up to see
Jack Frost leaning over the back of his
throne, glaring at them.

"Thieves!" he yelled.

He leaped over the back of the throne.

Rachel and Alicia zoomed out of his reach, but Kirsty wasn't quick enough. As she flew upward, he grabbed her arm in one bony hand and his cloak in the other. Kirsty was dragged down.

"Let me go!" she cried, struggling against him.

"Release my friend at once!" Alicia
demanded.

"No chance," said Jack Frost. "She's my
prisoner now!"

The three young fairies were staring in
shock, but none of them moved to help.

Rachel clenched her fists. She had to help her best friend! Suddenly, she had an idea.

"Kirsty, listen to me," she said in a loud voice. "Don't be scared—Jack Frost is a coward."

"What do you mean?" Kirsty called out.

"How dare you?" roared Jack Frost.

"He hasn't even tried to take the enchanted mirror out of his pocket," said Rachel with a laugh. "He's probably too scared to look in it!"

"I'm not scared of anything!" bellowed Jack Frost. "I'll show you!"

Still holding Kirsty with one hand, he managed to pull the mirror out of his cloak pocket. The cloak dropped to the floor, and Jack Frost gazed into the mirror.

At once, a confused look passed over his face. He frowned and shook his head a couple of times as if he felt dizzy. Jack Frost took a few steps forward and then stopped, as if he had forgotten what he was doing.

Rachel held her breath. Had the mirror worked?

Bad Is Good!

"Are you sure you want to hold on to that fairy?" Alicia asked Jack Frost.

"No way!" he said. He let go of Kirsty's arm, and she flew up to join Rachel and Alicia.

"He's getting confused between good and bad," Alicia whispered to the girls.

"That's great for us, because everything Jack Frost thinks is bad, we think is good!"

"Right," said Rachel in a determined voice. "Now I have a question for you, Jack Frost. Is it a good thing or a bad thing to give the enchanted mirror back to Alicia?"

"It's a good thing!" said Jack Frost in a puzzled voice.

Smiling, Alicia floated down and held out her hand. Jack Frost handed her

the mirror at once, although there was confusion in his eyes.

As soon as the mirror was in Alicia's hand, she held it up and cried out,

"Return all thoughts from wrong to right.
Correct the errors made tonight.
Winter winds bring ice and snow,
But stop Jack Frost
from bringing
woe."

The mirror gave a blue flash that lit up the whole room, and instantly the confusion left Jack Frost's eyes. The young fairies looked at one another in astonishment. Then the door burst open and the five other fairies darted in.

"Fly up!" Alicia called out, flinging the cloak over Jack Frost's head.

She seized the wands that had fallen

to the floor and
tossed them to
the fairies.
Everyone
shot upward,
and Jack
Frost
stumbled
around in
fury, trying
to tug the cloak off his head.

"You tricky fairy!" he bellowed. "I'll
make you sorry for this!"

With a flick of Alicia's wand, the young
fairies disappeared.

"I sent them back to the Fairyland
School, where they belong," she told the
girls with a smile. "You must go home,
too, but I promise to see you very soon!"

"You will never find the everlasting rose!" Jack Frost shrieked, dragging the cloak from his head and stomping on it. "My goblins have hidden it, and winter will last forever!"

"With my friends beside me, I can do anything!" Alicia declared.

She waved her wand again, and Rachel and Kirsty were caught up in a whirl of fairy dust as Alicia's magic whisked them home. They landed softly on their beds in Rachel's bedroom.

"What an adventure!" said Rachel, still a little out of breath.

"My head is still whirling!" Kirsty added with a laugh.

As usual, no time had passed since the girls had gone to Fairyland. Mrs. Walker's footsteps reached the top of the stairs, and the bedroom door opened.

"Goodnight, girls," she said with a smile. "Sweet dreams!"

"Thanks, Mom," Rachel said. The girls exchanged a secret smile. They knew that no dreams could be better than the amazing fairy adventure they had just shared!

The Everlasting Rose

Contents

Devious Divers

"I wish you didn't have to go home later," said Rachel, squeezing Kirsty's hand as they walked along. "I love it when you come to stay."

Kirsty smiled at her. The girls were in the park, taking Buttons for his morning walk. He was running back and forth, sniffing everything and wagging his tail.

"It's been a really magical visit so far," said Kirsty, as Buttons ran over to an empty flowerbed. "Meeting Alicia was amazing."

"Yes, it was," Rachel said, remembering Alicia's enchanted home. "I just hope we can help her find the third missing magical object."

"The everlasting rose," said Kirsty, nodding. "It sounds beautiful."

Rachel sighed as she looked at the flowerbeds that Buttons was sniffing.

"Without it, these flowerbeds will stay empty," she said. "Alicia said that her rose makes sure that new life is ready to burst out of the ground when spring comes. Winter will never end if we don't find it."

"That would ruin the cycle of the seasons," said Kirsty. "Every year is supposed to have spring, summer, fall, and winter. If it were winter all the time, people and animals would get sick, and plants wouldn't grow."

Rachel looked at the people in the park. Everyone looked pale, and no one was smiling. A couple of boys were walking away from the lake, carrying fishing rods.

"We can't fish when
the lake is frozen
over," the girls heard
one of them say. "I
don't like winter."

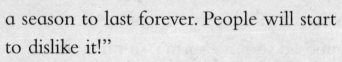

"Oh no," said
Rachel, feeling sad.
"Winter is a beautiful
season, but no one wants
a season to last forever. People will start
to dislike it!"

At that moment they were walking
toward a large cluster of bushes, thick
with frost. Just as they passed the bushes,
they both heard a squeaky, echoing giggle.
They stopped and stared at each other.

"Could that be . . . ?" said Kirsty.

"It sounded like . . . ," said Rachel.

"GOBLINS!" they exclaimed together.

The girls crouched down and peeked between the branches. A few feet away, there was an open space in the middle of the bushes, where three very strange figures were crowded together. They were wearing green diving suits with round, glass diving helmets.

"You sound really weird!" one of them was yelling.

His voice echoed as if he were shouting
in a tunnel. The others giggled and
bashed their helmets together.

"You look like green goldfish in a
bowl!" another goblin hooted, pointing at
the other two and laughing.

"Well, you look like a green blob,"
snapped the third goblin. "And you'll *still*
look like that when you take the diving
suit off, so there!"

The goblins lowered their voices.

"We have to get closer," Kirsty whispered. "They might know something about the everlasting rose."

The girls crawled into the bushes as quietly as they could. Now they could better hear what the goblins were saying. And they heard something that made them stare at each other in excitement.

"This time Jack Frost has thought of the best hiding place ever," the first goblin said. "There is no way that those pesky, goody-two-shoes fairies can get to the bottom of a frozen lake. Not even Alicia the Snow Queen Fairy can do that!"

Rachel and Kirsty shared a smile.

"Now we know exactly where to find the rose!" Kirsty whispered.

"Not *exactly*," Rachel replied. "The lake is really big. We have to know where to look."

Suddenly, there was a flurry of barks and Buttons came bounding into the bushes.

"Buttons, no!" Rachel whispered.

But Buttons had seen goblins before. If there was one thing he knew, it was that goblins were trouble, and he should get rid of them as quickly as possible.

"Run!" the goblins howled as Buttons charged toward them. "Protect the rose!"

The goblins scattered in multiple directions. Goblins were very scared of dogs—and of Buttons in particular!

Alicia Appears

Rachel managed to grab Buttons by the collar. She clipped on his leash and hugged him, shaking her head.

"Oh, Buttons, I know you think you're helping," she said. "But now the goblins will know that we are trying to get the rose back."

She led the panting dog out of the greenery, followed by Kirsty. The girls scrambled to their feet.

"Come on!" said Kirsty, grabbing Rachel's hand. "We have to stop one of those goblins and make him show us where the rose is hidden!"

Rachel and Kirsty sprinted toward the lake, with Buttons bounding along beside them. He thought it was all just a game, and was joining in with enthusiasm. He didn't understand everything about goblins and fairies,

but he knew one thing: Whenever
Rachel and Kirsty were together, there
were always great adventures to be had!

They skidded to a halt at the edge of
the ice-crusted lake and looked around.
Then Rachel let out a cry and pointed
to the opposite bank. The three goblins
were standing in a line, jostling with one
another to get in front. There was
a large, round hole in the
ice in front of them. As
the girls watched, the
goblins jumped through
the hole one by one
and disappeared
into the
deep lake.

Kirsty
groaned. "We

can't follow them in there! What are we going to do?"

"I have no idea," said Rachel, biting her lip. "Hey—what's that?"

A small speck was flying toward them across the lake.

"Is it Alicia?" Kirsty asked, her hopes rising.

"No, it's a bird," said Rachel. "I've never seen one like it before, though."

Kirsty stared at the bird as it flew toward them.

"Wow, I wish my dad could see this," she said. "He loves birds, and that's a really unusual one. I've only ever seen a picture of it in his bird book. It's called a snow bunting because of its white feathers."

"It's coming straight toward us," said

Rachel, feeling a little nervous. "Do snow buntings *like* humans?"

"It's going to crash into us!" Kirsty cried. "Duck!"

The girls dropped to the ground, and Buttons hid his head under his paws.

But when the snow bunting reached the bank where they were standing, it slowed down and landed on the edge of the lake. Rachel and Kirsty smiled and stood up. Sitting on the bird's back was the beautiful Snow Queen Fairy.

"Alicia!" they shouted together.

"Thank goodness you're here," Rachel added. "We know where the everlasting rose is!"

Alicia gave a delighted gasp and slipped off the back of the snow bunting. Her sparkling blue gown swirled around her as she kissed the bird.

"Thank you for bringing me here," she said. "You fly much faster than I do, my little friend."

The snow bunting twittered a good-bye and flew away across the park.

"Now, tell me everything," said Alicia.

She fluttered upward and hovered in front of the girls. Luckily, it was so cold that no one was walking around the lake, so there was no danger of her being seen.

"We saw three goblins wearing diving suits," Kirsty explained. "They were talking about how clever Jack Frost had been to hide the everlasting rose at the bottom of this lake."

"But the goblins saw us and ran off,"
Rachel continued. "So we followed them
here and watched them jump into the
lake through that hole. They've gone to
guard the rose."

She pointed at the hole, and Alicia
zoomed upward to get a better view.
When she floated back down, she looked
very upset.

"I can't fly underwater," she said. "Oh, girls, I think Jack Frost has defeated me!"

"Don't worry, Alicia! I'm sure we'll think of something," Kirsty said.

"Kirsty's right. We can't let Jack Frost win!" Rachel added.

Sparkling Skates

The girls could see that Alicia was starting to give up hope. Her shoulders slumped and she gazed down at the ground. Suddenly, Rachel thought of the boys they had seen earlier, carrying their fishing rods home.

"We can't go underwater," she said, "but perhaps we could fish for the rose.

Alicia, could you magic up a fishing rod for us?"

"I could," said Alicia, looking puzzled. "But if the goblins are guarding the rose, they can easily stop us from hooking it with a fishing rod."

"That's true," said Kirsty. "We'll have to get them out of the way somehow.

"You're right," Alicia replied. "With my magic and your wonderful ideas, we are unbeatable. We just need to think of something that will be more interesting to the goblins than guarding the rose."

Kirsty and Rachel exchanged amused glances. They knew the answer to this question.

"Snacks!" they said together.

All goblins loved snacks, and they usually found them impossible to resist.

Alicia waved her wand, and three clear
plastic snack boxes appeared on the
ground beside her. They each contained
a green cupcake, a bag of green cookies,
a bag of green-striped candy, some
green gummy treats, and a bag of
goblin-shaped chips. On the side of
each box were the words, DO NOT OPEN
UNDERWATER.

"Perfect!"
exclaimed
Rachel,
clapping
her hands
together.

Alicia gave
another little
flick of her
wand, and a

fishing rod appeared in Kirsty's hand.
Rachel picked up the snack boxes and
looked across at the
hole.

"It's going to
take us forever
to walk around
the lake to the
other side," she
said.

But Alicia
smiled. She raised
her wand for a third
time and recited a spell.

"Come snow, come ice, do not delay,
Or cruel Jack Frost will win the day.
Help me now, for winter's sake,
And speed my friends across the lake."

Instantly, both of the girls realized they were wearing a pair of glittering skates.

"They are made of ice," said Alicia with a smile. "They will last just long enough to get you to the other side of the lake, and then they will melt away."

"Wait here, Buttons," said Rachel.

Buttons sat down, and then Kirsty and Rachel stepped onto the ice, feeling nervous and excited at the same time. But they didn't need to worry. The skates were perfectly shaped for their feet, and soon they were gliding across the frozen lake, striking out toward the hole where the goblins had disappeared.

"This is so much fun!" Kirsty exclaimed happily.

Even though they were worried about the everlasting rose, both girls were thrilled by the *swish-swish* of their magical skates on the ice and the cold wind on their cheeks. The journey was over too quickly, and soon they were stepping onto the bank on the other side. Alicia had flown ahead and was already waiting for them there.

"That was wonderful," said Rachel in a breathless voice.

As she spoke, her ice skates melted away into nothing. Kirsty's did the same.

"I'm glad you enjoyed it," said Alicia. "Skating is one of the most enchanting things about winter."

Rachel took the end of the fishing line and hooked it onto one of the snack boxes. Then Kirsty carried the fishing rod over to the hole in the ice. She dropped the box into the freezing water and let it sink downward.

"I think it's reached the bottom," she said after a few moments. "Oh! Something is tugging on the line!"

"Hold on tight!" Rachel cried. "Don't let it get away!"

A Fishing Trip

Kirsty turned the reel handle, and the
fishing rod bent as it pulled on something
heavy.

"It's coming!" said Kirsty.

Then, with a splash and spray of water,
one of the goblins shot out through the
hole and landed on the bank. He was
clinging to the snack box. As the girls

141

watched, he tore off his helmet, opened
the box, and started to munch on the
food. Then he noticed Alicia, Rachel,
and Kirsty, and his eyes opened wide.
His mouth was so full that he couldn't
say a word.

"Home you go!" Alicia sang out.

She waved her wand, and the goblin
vanished in a flurry of sparkling
snowflakes.

"One down, two to go," said Rachel. "Time to go fishing again, Kirsty!"

The second snack box went underwater, and exactly the same thing happened. The second goblin was sent back home, still munching his snacks. Kirsty sent the third box down through the hole, and soon the fishing rod started to bend again.

"I've got him," she said. "As soon as he is safely out of the way, we can fish for the everlasting rose."

But this time, when the goblin came shooting out of the water, he wasn't just holding a snack box. Tucked under his other arm was a sealed glass box, and inside the box was the most beautiful rose that the girls had ever seen. Its velvety petals were deep red, and there

were drops of dew clinging to its delicate
leaves. It looked as if it had just been
picked.

"My rose!" Alicia exclaimed.

Her voice sounded loving and worried
at the same time. The goblin pulled
off his helmet, stuffed half the cupcake
into his mouth, and gave them all an
unpleasant grin.

"I knew there was some fairy trickery going on," he said, spitting cupcake crumbs everywhere as he spoke.

"It's rude to talk with your mouth full," said Kirsty. "Almost as rude as taking things that don't belong to you."

The goblin ignored her. He was far too busy feeling pleased with himself.

"I'm so smart!" he boasted. "I guessed that one of those pesky fairies was sending the snacks down, but I was the only goblin who thought of a way to keep the rose safe *and* eat my snacks!"

"Give the rose back to Alicia," said Rachel. "It doesn't belong to you."

"Are you kidding?" asked the goblin in an impertinent tone. "I'm taking the rose straight back to Jack Frost, so he can see how wonderful I am. Then he'll choose another hiding place—one that you will *never* find!"

Suddenly, Kirsty remembered Jack Frost reading *The Snow Queen* to the goblins. She thought of the puzzle that the Snow Queen used to keep little Kay a prisoner, and that gave her an idea.

"You're right," she said. "You have been very smart. You've been too smart for us—we never thought that you might take the everlasting rose away with you."

The goblin puffed out his chest, and Alicia looked at Kirsty in surprise. But Rachel smiled—she could always tell when her best friend had a plan!

"Before you go, we have something that you might find interesting," Kirsty went on. "It's an ice puzzle, but only someone who is really, really smart will be able to complete it. Would you like to give it a try?"

She winked at Alicia, who was holding
her wand behind her back. She gave it
a little shake, and there was a tinkling
sound like falling glass. Nine large pieces
of ice thumped onto the ground in front
of the goblin.

"It's a magical ice jigsaw puzzle," Alicia explained. "The pieces look blank now, but when they are all put together, your face will appear on the puzzle."

Looking excited, the goblin started to try to fit the pieces together. But he kept dropping them because his arms were so full.

"Maybe you should put the snack box down," Rachel suggested.

Nodding, the goblin set the snack box down beside him. But it was very difficult to hold on to the large pieces of ice with just one hand.

"Oh, bother!" he squawked as another one slipped out of his grasp.

"You need both hands free to concentrate on this puzzle," said Kirsty.

"Why don't you put your other box down, too?"

She held her breath. She could see the goblin hesitating. Would he fall for her trick?

The Magic of Winter

"Good idea," said the goblin.

He placed the glass box on top of the snack box and turned back to the puzzle. At once, Alicia zoomed around behind him and tapped the box with her wand. It melted away, and the rose simply floated into her arms. It shrank to fairy size as she touched it, and a huge smile

spread across her face.
Rachel and Kirsty
shared a hug
and jumped
up and down
in excitement.

"We did it!"
said Alicia,
flying across
and giving each
of them a tiny kiss on
the cheek. "Thank you, from the bottom
of my heart!"

The fragrant scent of the everlasting
rose surrounded them as they smiled at
one another.

"Done!" crowed the goblin, putting
his hands on his hips proudly. "See how
smart I am?"

He had completed the ice puzzle, and his own face gazed up at him from the finished design. But as he looked at it, the puzzle face rolled its eyes and shook its head. He frowned, looked up, and saw Alicia holding her rose.

"It's time for you to go home," she said to him. "Tell Jack Frost that my friends and I will never allow him to ruin winter."

She sounded as regal as a queen, and
the goblin gulped. Before he could say
a word, Alicia waved her wand and sent
him back to Fairyland.

"Now I must
take the rose
back where
it belongs,"
she went on,
fluttering in
front of the
girls.

"We'll never
forget our amazing
adventures with you," said Rachel,
smiling at the little fairy.

"Winter will always seem even more
magical from now on," Kirsty added.

"I hope so," said Alicia. "I will never

forget you, either. Good-bye, Rachel! Good-bye, Kirsty!"

The girls waved as Alicia vanished back to her snowy Fairyland home.

"We'd better start walking," said Rachel. "Buttons is waiting for us on the other side of the lake."

They set off arm in arm, and then something beautiful happened. The gray clouds parted, and a shaft of bright winter sunlight broke through. It lit up one of the park's empty flowerbeds, and the girls smiled at each other.

"It's funny," said Kirsty. "The flowerbeds look just the same, but everything is different now that Alicia has her magical objects back. We know that the seeds and bulbs are growing under the soil, and new life is getting ready for springtime."

Rachel nodded. "Winter is a beautiful season," she said. "But knowing that it will end makes it even more special. Now everyone can enjoy the snowy weather and feel glad that spring is coming, too."

"So what do you think is the best thing about winter?" Kirsty asked.

Rachel laughed happily. "That's easy," she said. "Fairy adventures, of course!"

RAINBOW magic
THE STORYBOOK FAIRIES

Rachel and Kirsty found Alicia's missing
magical objects. Now it's time for
them to help...

Elle
the Thumbelina Fairy!

Join their next adventure in this
special sneak peek...

Into the Pages

The other fairies jumped up and smiled at Rachel and Kirsty.

"It's wonderful to meet you," Rachel said, recovering from the surprise of being whisked to Fairyland. "But why have you brought us here?"

"I'm afraid that Jack Frost and his goblins have done something truly terrible," said Elle, sinking into one of the chairs.

She raised her wand and pointed it at one of the bookshelves. A large book swept itself off the shelf and opened in midair to a big, blank page. As it hovered there, blurry pictures began to appear on the page. As the pictures grew clearer and the girls drew in their breaths.

"It's a picture of this library," said Kirsty.

"With Jack Frost and his goblins sneaking around inside," Rachel added. "What did they do?"

"They took our most precious belongings," said Elle.

The girls watched the picture in the book. Jack Frost undid the golden clasp of a wooden box. He raised the lid and scooped the contents into a bag, laughing. Then he handed the bag to a goblin, threw the box on the floor, and left the library.

The picture faded, and the book closed itself and slotted back into its place on the shelf.

"What was in the box?" asked Rachel.

"Four magical objects that have power over the stories we protect," said Elle. "They give the holder control of the stories. We use them to make sure that the stories go as they are supposed to, so every story ends happily."

"What is Jack Frost using them for?" Kirsty asked.

"He and his goblins are using our magical objects to actually go *into* the stories and change them," said Elle. "They want the stories to be all about them."

Kirsty and Rachel exchanged a worried glance.

RAINBOW magic™

Which Magical Fairies Have You Met?

- ❑ The Rainbow Fairies
- ❑ The Weather Fairies
- ❑ The Jewel Fairies
- ❑ The Pet Fairies
- ❑ The Sports Fairies
- ❑ The Ocean Fairies
- ❑ The Princess Fairies
- ❑ The Superstar Fairies
- ❑ The Fashion Fairies
- ❑ The Sugar & Spice Fairies
- ❑ The Earth Fairies
- ❑ The Magical Crafts Fairies
- ❑ The Baby Animal Rescue Fairies
- ❑ The Fairy Tale Fairies
- ❑ The School Day Fairies

◣SCHOLASTIC

Find all of your favorite fairy friends at
scholastic.com/rainbowmagic

RMFAIRY15

SPECIAL EDITION

Which Magical Fairies Have You Met?

❏ Joy the Summer Vacation Fairy
❏ Holly the Christmas Fairy
❏ Kylie the Carnival Fairy
❏ Stella the Star Fairy
❏ Shannon the Ocean Fairy
❏ Trixie the Halloween Fairy
❏ Gabriella the Snow Kingdom Fairy
❏ Juliet the Valentine Fairy
❏ Mia the Bridesmaid Fairy
❏ Flora the Dress-Up Fairy
❏ Paige the Christmas Play Fairy
❏ Emma the Easter Fairy
❏ Cara the Camp Fairy
❏ Destiny the Rock Star Fairy
❏ Belle the Birthday Fairy
❏ Olympia the Games Fairy

❏ Selena the Sleepover Fairy
❏ Cheryl the Christmas Tree Fairy
❏ Florence the Friendship Fairy
❏ Lindsay the Luck Fairy
❏ Brianna the Tooth Fairy
❏ Autumn the Falling Leaves Fairy
❏ Keira the Movie Star Fairy
❏ Addison the April Fool's Day Fairy
❏ Bailey the Babysitter Fairy
❏ Natalie the Christmas Stocking Fairy
❏ Lila and Myla the Twins Fairies
❏ Chelsea the Congratulations Fairy
❏ Carly the School Fairy
❏ Angelica the Angel Fairy
❏ Blossom the Flower Girl Fairy
❏ Skyler the Fireworks Fairy
❏ Giselle the Christmas Ballet Fairy

■ SCHOLASTIC

Find all of your favorite fairy friends at
scholastic.com/rainbowmagic

3 stories in each one!

HIT entertainment

RMSPECIAL19